WALTER BROWN AND THE MAGICIAN'S HAT

KAREN INGLIS

Illustrated by
DAMIR KUNDALIĆ

~WS~
Well Said Press

MAGICAL BONUS EDITION!

Includes Chapters 1 & 2 of **The Secret Lake**
and **Eeek! The Runaway Alien**

Both top sellers at school events.
We'd hate you to miss out!

ISBN: 978-0-9569323-8-9
wellsaidpress.com

FOR EVERYONE WHO BELIEVES IN MAGIC

1

THE BIRTHDAY SURPRISE

As dawn broke on the morning of Walter Brown's tenth birthday he hadn't the faintest idea that his life was about to change forever. Like most other boys his age he was still fast asleep in bed.

The wall beside him was covered with posters showing distant galaxies and planets, the sun, the moon and, of course, Earth. On the opposite wall hung a poster of his favourite football team, Southbridge Wanderers, and a team photo from his local soccer club. Walter, meanwhile, lay flat on his back underneath his duvet, only his gentle breathing stirring the still morning air.

Despite appearances, astronomy and football were the furthest things from Walter's mind at this precise moment. So, for that matter, was his tenth birthday.

Walter was far too busy dreaming his favourite dream — the one where he was in the circus ring with Great-grandpa Horace, helping him perform magic.

As ever, the benches all around brimmed with row upon row of smiling faces disappearing high into the shadows of the Big Top. As always, the smiling faces were all screaming and shouting, 'More, Grandpa Horace! More!'

And now, as in every dream, Great-grandpa Horace turned slowly to Walter in his black top hat and gave him a friendly wink. 'Let's do the last trick again shall we, Walter?' The audience cheered as Walter gave a broad grin, picked up a silver-tipped wand from the table in front of him and passed it into his great-grandpa's tiny white-gloved hands.

In fact, Walter had never met Great-grandpa Horace. He had died when Walter was a baby. But his mum had an old box full of newspaper cuttings, and black and white photographs taken during the 50 years he had spent travelling around Europe with the circus. His tricks were so unusual they made headline news in every city he visited — like the time he turned a horse into a snake, or when he managed to magic sweets into the hands of all the children in the audience, and another time when he made someone's dad vanish and reappear on the other side of the Big Top.

The newspapers said they'd heard that even the Magic Circle couldn't explain how he did it but, being very secretive (and probably a bit jealous), they would never comment.

At the age of five Walter announced he wanted to be a magician. And though astronomy and football had since taken over, his fascination with magic had never quite left him.

Had Walter been awake just now, he might have wondered why his dream had returned so vividly this particular morning. But, of course, he wasn't and so he dreamed on — for a short while at least.

A clock downstairs chimed once. Moments later

Walter's door creaked open, shedding a beam of light from the hallway across the floor and onto his bed. A tall, fluffy, black tail passed silently through the doorway. The owner of the proud tail, which now glided serenely across the room towards Walter's bed, was Walter's cat, Sixpence.

The creak of the door and the shaft of light had already begun to stir Walter. When Sixpence jumped onto his bed Walter turned over and groaned as small lumpy paws padded over his legs, across his ribs and up towards his head. The loud purring in his ear was the final straw.

'Oh, Sixpence! It's the middle of the night,' Walter mumbled in a sleepy grump. 'Why can't you just stay on the mattress and off me? Now settle down and go to sleep.'

'*Not* on your life,' retorted Sixpence (except that Walter couldn't hear her). 'I've been waiting for this moment for five years!'

Sixpence continued purring loudly, then started nudging her head repeatedly against Walter's ear.

'Come on, Walter. Wake up — it's your birthday! We've got things to do!'

Despite the nudging and the purring, and even a bit of licking, Walter was already falling back into a deep sleep. 'I don't believe this,' cried Sixpence. 'It's the boy's tenth birthday, the most important one of his life, and all he wants to do is sleep!'

Sixpence leapt off the bed, and stalked over to a pile of presents in the corner of the room. She sat down, took in an enormous breath, and let out a loud, grating 'Miauowww!' It worked. Walter sat up in bed rubbing his eyes.

'Are you all right, Sixpence?' he croaked, half asleep and half cross. But then, peering over, he saw the pile of presents in the grey morning light and remembered. 'Hey! It's my birthday! Well *done*, Sixpence!'

Walter scrambled out of his bed across to Sixpence.

He glanced at his bedside clock and groaned — it was only just gone 6.30 and no one would be up before 8. He thought about waiting (for about two seconds), but the temptation was too great.

Walter ripped the packaging off the first present. His face lit up. 'Wow! Southbridge Wanderers' new football strip. *Very* nice!' He held the red and white striped shirt up against himself and tried a few air kicks with his bare feet.

He tore the wrapping off the next present — a junior chemistry set. *Create a world of fizzing and exploding science experiments right in your own home!* said the blurb on the front of the box.

'Awesome!' said Walter, his eyes wide as he studied the list of contents and experiments. (His dad was chemistry teacher at the local college — no prizes for guessing whose idea this was.)

As he picked up the next present Sixpence meowed loudly and flicked her tail from side to side. '*Nooo!* Not that one!' she said (unheard), instead peering hard at a tall rectangular box at the back of the pile.

'Hey, it's from Todd,' said Walter, beaming. He'd recognise that handwriting anywhere. He blinked and swallowed hard. It had only been three weeks since his best friend had moved from next door, but already it felt like a year. 'Wow! A book on the Northern Lights,' he whispered as the paper fell away.

'B-o-r-i-n-g!' said Sixpence with a yawn as Walter began to leaf through the pages, gasping at each new photograph.

But then the cat's black fluffy fur began to bristle and stand on end as Walter finally reached to the back of the pile for the tall box with the silver paper.

Walter tore at the wrapping, adding it to the growing pile, which now surrounded Sixpence. The last piece of paper fell to the ground to reveal a battered purple box with the words *Handle With Care* written in faded black ink diagonally across its side.

'I wonder what this is, Sixpence?' Walter held the box at eye level and shook it gently from side to side. Something inside rattled. He sniffed the box. It was definitely old — like the inside of a wardrobe that hadn't been opened for 20 years. 'Time to find out!' he said eagerly.

Walter placed the box on his desk and pulled up the dog-eared flaps that criss-crossed over the top end.

As he peered down inside he took a quick inward breath as he found himself staring at a slightly tatty black top hat.

'Check this out!' he cried. Carefully, he reached in
and lifted out the hat. As he did so, a slip of yellow paper
fluttered out unnoticed and landed on the carpet.

Sixpence moved to take a sitting position beside it.

Still holding the hat aloft, Walter peered inside the
box. At the bottom, previously hidden by the hat, lay a
pair of white-grey gloves. But that wasn't all. Wedged
along one side, held in with a metal wire, was a faded
black stick with a silver end.

Walter's heart began to race. He placed the top hat
carefully on his bed and, with arms trembling, lifted out
the gloves and slipped them on. Then he unhooked the
stick from its resting place.

'A magician's outfit,' he breathed, his mouth widening into a smile. He held up the wand between his white-gloved fingers and turned to reach for the hat. As he did so, he spotted the square of yellow paper on the carpet beside Sixpence.

'What's that, Sixpence?' He leaned forward, picked up the note and quickly unfolded it. The message in looped and shaky handwriting was addressed to him:

For my great and only grandson, Walter Brown. A gift on your 10th birthday, which was a gift to me on mine. It's a magical age! Stay focused and have fun!

Sorry I can't be there to see you open this!

With love from your late, Great-grandpa Horace xx

2

A TALKING CAT

'Wow, Sixpence!' said Walter, picking up the hat. 'It's from Great-grandpa Horace!'

'*Now* we're talking,' said Sixpence (still unheard). 'Well, go on — go and put it on then!'

Walter picked up the hat and carried it carefully towards his mirror. Slowly and ceremoniously he lifted it above his head (about ten centimetres), then lowered it on.

'That looks fantastic!' cried Sixpence.

'Thanks!' said Walter, beaming. '*Now*—'

Walter freeze-framed and glanced at his cat's reflection in the mirror. 'D-Did you just… *say* something?' he asked, his eyes popping. But then he immediately felt ridiculous and snorted a half chuckle.

'Sure!' cried Sixpence. 'I said the hat looks fantastic!'

Walter grasped his hat by the brim, stepped two paces back, and fell flat on his back on his bed.

'And by the way I'm "Sixth Sense", *not* Sixpence!' said Sixth Sense with a sigh. 'Have you any idea what it's like being called the wrong name for *five whole years?!*'

Walter slowly sat up, his mouth wide open, his eyes saucer-like. He tried to speak but the words stuck tight.

'Come on, Walter — get a grip!' said Sixth Sense. 'We've got things to do before the grown-ups wake. Now, *please*, close your mouth and get that ridiculous expression off your face!'

Walter jerked out of his trance and snapped his mouth shut. 'Now hang on a minute,' he said indignantly. 'You've got some explaining to do. You can't just expect me to wake up on my tenth birthday and start *talking* to my cat — who, by the way, I find *rather* rude.'

'Typical curious young boy!' said Sixth Sense, parading around the room with her tail in the air. 'Mind you, curiosity is no bad thing — not *even* for us cats.' She stopped and twisted to lick the top of her back left leg. 'In fact,' she continued, looking back up at Walter, 'it's just what the doctor ordered.'

'Pardon?' said Walter. 'If you're going to talk in riddles we might as well forget it!' He reached to remove his hat.

'Don't do that!' said Sixth Sense. She flashed her green eyes. 'You won't hear me.'

'*Sor-ry,*' said Walter slowly. Then, still clutching the hat brim, he narrowed his eyes and grinned at his cat mischievously. 'In that case don't *tempt* me to take it off! Now, tell me what's going on.'

Sixth Sense stretched out her front legs and pushed her bottom and tail into the air.

'Okay, okay,' she said, clawing at the carpet as Walter looked on with a frown, 'I suppose I do owe you an explanation now we've officially become partners.'

'*Partners?*'

'Yes, Walter, partners. You and me!'

She came out of her stretch and sat down, then lifted her left paw and started washing her face.

'Can you stop doing that, please?' said Walter crossly.

'Okay, okay.' She placed her paw back down and looked up at Walter.

'Well,' she began, 'it all started when I was born. I was the sixth in the litter and early on my mother spotted I was special.' She stood up and began stalking around the room, tail high again. 'Of course, everyone knows we cats have a sixth sense. You know, *sensing* when something's about to happen.' She narrowed her eyes. 'Telephones ringing, doorbells going, that sort of stuff.

'In that way we are, of course, *superior* to you humans,' she added, darting a sideways glance at Walter.

'*Superior!* That's a bit cheeky!' scoffed Walter.

'Anyway, I was born with an unusually strong dose of *numero* six,' Sixth Sense went on, '— to the extent that I see happenings far in the future as well. That's how I knew about Great-grandpa Horace's present.'

'*What?*' Walter's eyebrows shot up. 'You mean you *knew* Great-grandpa Horace would give me a magician's outfit today?'

'Of course I did! I've known since the day your mum bought me from that lady at the mobile library. And there's something else...'

'Go on...' said Walter slowly. Surely nothing could surprise him now.

Sixth Sense's green eyes seemed to glow with pride. 'Well, Walter, I can also see into the past. And it turns out that my great-great-great...' She paused and shook her head. 'Actually, I lose count of how many greats. But my great-whatever-number-it-is grandmother belonged to — your great-grandpa!'

Walter's mouth fell open. '*What?* You're descended from my great-grandpa's cat?'

'Yep!' said Sixth Sense triumphantly.

'How...? W... W...' Walter struggled to push his words out.

'Well,' said Sixth Sense, 'when your great-grandpa went away with the circus he gave my great-great etc etc

grandma to a woman who ran a *perambulating* library.'
She narrowed her eyes. 'That's a mobile library to you.'

She continued. 'And my great-great-whatever-the-
number-is grandma went on to have kittens who had
more kittens and so on, and over the years they got
passed to the owners and customers of that library and
other mobile libraries. And that's where you come in,
Walter, because you're the one who persuaded your
mum to rescue me from that awful, fussy woman at
your mobile library. And what a relief that was, I can
tell you!'

She glanced at the ceiling and seemed to shudder.

Walter re-played the story in his mind, clearly
picturing the morning he'd tugged at his mum's hand and

pleaded with her to take one of the kittens the lady had for sale in the basket under her desk. He'd picked Sixpence because he liked her name and the look in her eyes. He was only five then, but right now it felt like yesterday.

Sixth Sense leapt onto the bed, interrupting his daydream. 'So, you see, Walter, we've been *chosen* — you and me!' Her green eyes lit up. *'Isn't it exciting?'*

'Chosen? Chosen for what?' Walter, still trying to take in everything Sixth Sense had said, had started to dress himself. He wasn't sure he was ready for yet more surprises.

'I'm not sure.' The cat squinted thoughtfully up at the window. 'All I know is it involves travelling abroad.'

'Abroad…?' Walter heard himself reply in a high voice.

'I don't know when or where, or *what* exactly happens,' Sixth Sense went on, 'but what I do know is that your great-grandpa has something to do with it and you'll need to perform magic when the time comes. That means we must get some practice in — and *pronto!'* She narrowed her eyes. 'That's *soon* to you.'

Walter's eyes started to glaze over as he pictured himself performing magic in a distant land in Great-grandpa Horace's outfit. Was he destined to follow in his footsteps around the cities of Europe, making the headlines with his magic tricks? If he were, that really *would* be a dream come true!

'Ahem!' said Sixth Sense.

'Ooops — sorry!' said Walter, coming out of his trance. 'Okay, …er…practice. So, where do we start?'

'Well,' said Sixth Sense, pacing up and down, 'how about something close to home?'

'Like what?'

Sixth Sense paused, then slipped him a sideways glance. 'Like the Braithwaite twins up in Cotswolds Close?'

'What — Harry and George?' Walter tried to sound casual but already his heart was fluttering. The twins had moved into one of the big new houses at the top of the road the week before Todd moved out. Their dad rode a Harley Davidson and worked in film and, according to Todd, their mum was a famous actress (or at least someone else had told Todd that). Walter was dying to meet them but hadn't yet plucked up the courage to knock on their door in case it looked like sucking up. He'd even thought about asking them to his birthday party, but had got cold feet when he started writing out the invitation — they just seemed so much cooler than him.

'That's right, Harry and George,' said Sixth Sense.

'Perhaps you could impress them with some magic? I know you've been dying to meet them.'

Walter shot a startled look at her. 'Hey, how did you know that? You're not a mind-reader too, are you?'

'Not exactly,' said Sixth Sense. 'But I pick up on a lot that's going on around me — sorry, partner, can't help it.' She sighed. 'Usually happens when I'm falling asleep — most annoying!'

Walter felt his cheeks flush. He just hoped that Sixth Sense couldn't pick up on *all* of his thoughts.

'Okay, so all we need is a plan,' said Sixth Sense. 'Any thoughts?'

Walter tapped his chin with his forefinger. 'Well, if I had a dad with a Harley Davidson, a mum who was a film actress and my own personal cinema room with a 75-inch TV, I think I'd need a **lot** of impressing. Do you really think I'm up to this, Sixth Sense? I mean, I don't want to make an idiot of myself!'

Unnoticed by Walter, Sixth Sense's fur had begun to stand on end.

'That cinema room of theirs is pretty awesome,' Walter went on, adjusting his hat in the mirror. 'You can practically watch their screen from the other side of the street it's so big! And they've got *really* cool games, not that Todd and I spied on them or anythi—'

Sixth Sense sprang to the ground, her green eyes sparkling. 'Television! *Brilliant* idea, Walter!'

'*Pardon?*' Walter furrowed his brow as he stared at his cat.

'Now, listen carefully,' said Sixth Sense, 'I happen to know that Harry and George will be putting on their new *Planet Voss Monster Battle* game at just after 10 o'clock this morning. Why don't we try out some magic on that?'

Butterfly nerves began tickling inside Walter's tummy but he instantly willed them away. He was curious to know whether he could really make magic happen and his heart beat fast at the prospect. (The butterfly thing always happened with a dare — like the time Todd dared him to jump off his shed roof. It had taken Walter all of ten seconds to quell his nerves — thanks to a TV programme he'd once seen called *Mind Over Matter*. And a brilliant jump it had been too!)

'Now, you're the gaming expert,' said Sixth Sense. 'What magic trick would you like to try on their game?'

Walter frowned. 'Wow, I dunno. What have I got to choose from?'

'Anything you like, partner. That's why it's called magic!'

Walter thought hard, but try as he might his mind

remained stubbornly blank — like a switched off TV in fact.

Thirty seconds ticked by.

'I've got it!' cried Sixth Sense, jerking Walter out of his trance. 'Why don't we spirit away all of the game monsters?'

Walter raised his eyebrows in horror. 'That would be stealing!' he gasped. 'We can't do that!'

'Of course we can, partner. It's magic, not stealing! Besides Great-grandpa Horace did say, "Have fun"!'

Sixth Sense brushed against Walter's lower legs, her tail in the air. 'Your birthday party's not until this afternoon, Walter, so we've got time this morning to try it.'

A smile began spreading across Walter's face — then froze. 'Hang on a minute! If the twins *know* I've performed magic, then my secret's out, isn't it? I can't have the whole town knowing I'm a real magician, can I? They might take Great-grandpa Horace's things away from me! Where's the *sixth sense* in that?' He rolled his eyes and shook his head.

'Darn it!' Sixth Sense lowered her tail and sat down. 'Sorry, Walter, got a bit carried away there. *Devil's in the detail*, as my mother used to say.'

She cocked her head to one side and gazed at the window, deep in thought. 'Ha!' she said. 'Why don't we do it from across the road? You said you can see their TV from outside, right?'

Walter nodded, but then started to frown, realising this meant he wouldn't get to meet the twins after all.

'What's more,' Sixth Sense went on, 'this way we can get Harry and George to come out and meet you without you having to suck up and knock on their door!'

'How does *that* work?' said Walter, blushing as he realised Sixth Sense had picked up on the sucking-up thing from his thoughts.

'All will become clear — trust me, partner! You get to practise your magic in secret. *And* you get to meet the twins.' Sixth Sense stood up and started to parade around the room again.

Walter pulled his great grandfather's note from his jeans pocket and read it again. Slowly he started to grin. Sixth Sense was right — this would be fun. If the trick worked, the boys would probably just think they'd unlocked a new level in their game. And if it didn't, he wouldn't have made an idiot of himself in front of them. Either way he'd get to meet Harry and George, Sixth Sense had promised. What could possibly go wrong?

Walter splayed out his fingers and pulled each of his white gloves farther up his wrists. 'Perfect!' he said, turning to look at himself in the mirror. He picked up his wand, held it aloft and tapped the side of his hat with it three times for luck. He just hoped that his Great-grandpa Horace would approve of their plan.

'Happy birthday, darling. Wow — you've been busy!'
Walter swung round to see his mother standing in his doorway in her dressing gown.

'Oh, er...hi, Mum.' His mind blanked and his cheeks began to burn. In panic, he glanced at Sixth Sense who looked every inch a normal cat.
'Well, go on, *say* something!' said Sixth Sense impatiently.
'Morning, Sixpence!' said Walter's mother, beaming.

Walter gulped in panic, waiting for the cat's reply — but none came.

'Gosh, th-thanks for all the great presents!' The heat from Walter's cheeks subsided as he realised that his mother hadn't heard a word his cat had uttered.

'S-Sorry for not waiting,' he stuttered. 'Sixpence woke me up and I couldn't get back to sleep.'

His mum chuckled. 'That's fine, darling. I'd have done exactly the same on *my* tenth birthday if I'd woken up early!'

'Can you *believe* Great-grandpa Horace's magician's outfit?' said Walter, holding up his wand and tapping his hat.

'I certainly can. He told us he was going to leave it to you on the day you were born. You were the only boy in his family you know, Walter — just daughters and granddaughters before that. But he made us promise to keep it a surprise until your tenth birthday. It looks great!'

Walter thought for a moment. 'Did he ever have a cat?' he asked, darting a glance at Sixth Sense.

'I've no idea. What a funny question, Walter! Now, come and show your outfit to Dad.' Walter's mum turned into the hall. 'By the way,' she said over her shoulder, 'were you talking to yourself just now?'

Walter's cheeks started to tingle again. 'Er, well, sort

of,' he replied in a high voice. 'Just practising my first tricks!'

'Out of the way now, Sixpence!' Walter's mother raised her left foot and nudged the cat out of her path with the tip of her slipper.

Sixth Sense scowled and shot ahead down the hall as Walter tried not to smirk.

3

PRACTICE MISSION

'**A**re you really going to go out dressed like that?' said Sixth Sense.

It was just before 10 o'clock and Walter stood beside his bed wearing his red and white striped Southbridge Wanderers top, a pair of jeans, and his top hat. A white glove poked out of each pocket and he twirled his wand in circles with his right hand.

'How else are we meant to talk?' said Walter. 'Besides, it's my birthday outfit — sort of. Not a bad cover if you ask me...'

He grinned wickedly, then fell backwards onto his bed and pointed the wand at his cat. 'Anyway, don't you go poking fun at me, or I just *might* wave my magician's wand at you!'

Sixth Sense jumped back, her eyes sparkling.

Walter's wristwatch bleeped twice from his bedside table. It was 10 o'clock. 'It's time, partner,' said Sixth Sense.

Walter's heart skipped several beats. He went to stand up again, but couldn't. His legs suddenly felt like jelly and his stomach began churning, as if an army of butterflies and moths were flying around inside, all bumping into each other. He tried willing them away but it didn't seem to be working.

'Sixth Sense, I don't think I can do this. I feel sick!' he said suddenly.

'Nonsense! Of course you can!' Sixth Sense stalked across the room towards the door. 'Follow me, do as I say, and everything will be all right. Once you get a taste of your new powers there'll be no stopping you!'

Walter forced himself off the bed and followed Sixth Sense down the stairs.

'I'm just going to pick up my soccer magazine,' he called from the hall in a high voice (it always did that when he was nervous or lying).

The newsagent's was at the bottom of the road — usually his favourite place to go with Todd on a Saturday morning to spend their pocket money. He sighed inside, remembering last week's trip. It just wasn't the same going on his own.

'Hey, Walter, any chance of some magic to help me get my homework done faster? I've got *so* much to get through!' Walter's big sister Hannah appeared behind him in the hall with a pile of books in her arms.

Walter turned and waved his wand in a quick circle, then pulled a goofy smile at her as he reached for the door. Hannah didn't miss much these days, and if he opened his mouth again she'd know something was up.

To his relief she just crossed her eyes in reply — like she used to when they were younger.

Walter stepped outside, Sixth Sense at his heels, and slammed the door behind him. Then, complete with tummy butterflies and moths, and a talking cat, headed not down the road to the newsagent's, but up the hill towards Cotswolds Close and the home of Harry and George Braithwaite.

4

BROTHERLY BRAWL

As the clock struck ten in the cinema room at number 14 Cotswolds Close, twins Harry and George Braithwaite, aged 11, and their younger brother, Thomas, aged five and three-quarters, sat watching *Batman*. A huge, sleek TV screen hung on the wall opposite. On a shelf below stood a row of silver-framed photographs of their parents at different film parties. High definition surround sound filled the room.

At two minutes past ten, Harry, the older twin with the slightly darker curly hair, hit the 'stop' button. 'We've seen this too many times. Let's play *Planet Voss* instead,' he said.

'Great idea!' said George, his brown eyes widening.

'No way! I want to watch the rest of *Batman*!' said

little Thomas, in a cross, loud voice (he'd learned that this worked better than shouting).

'Sorry, Tom. Two against one!' said Harry quickly.

He tossed the remote control into George's lap and dived across the room towards the games console.

Harry often spoke in haste, and usually before thinking. Their mum said this was because he'd shot into the world first at record speed and was wailing even before the doctors had cut the cord. George, by contrast, had kept everyone waiting fifteen minutes after his brother's arrival and had needed three bottom slaps before he cried. This probably explained why George always paused before speaking — and often found himself fixing problems caused by Harry's haste.

'We only watched *Batman* the other night,' George said gently, as tears brimmed in his little brother's eyes. 'Anyway, you love *Planet Voss*, Tom!'

Unfortunately, George's approach didn't always work — and this was one such time. With his nostrils flaring and cheeks reddening, Thomas jumped up and tried to yank the remote control from his older brother.

Harry, taking advantage of the distraction, quickly slipped the *Planet Voss* game into the machine. At the sound of the click Thomas burst into tears and tugged even harder at the remote. But as soon as the *Planet Voss Monster*

Battle music began to play, and the first images appeared on the screen, he abandoned his struggle. Then, seeing the White Crystal Warriors preparing for battle, he dried his tears, reached for a chocolate biscuit from the coffee table, and sat down between his two brothers to watch the game.

At around the same time as Harry hit 'stop' on the *Batman* film, Sixth Sense and Walter were leaving the house. 'Boy, are they in for a surprise!' Sixth Sense said as they set off up the road.

Walter, gradually feeling less sick, started practising waving his wand in the air. 'Whoosh, whoosh,' he whispered as he swept it back and forth and in circles in front of him. As they neared the Braithwaites' house he suddenly stopped and looked down at his cat with a frown.

'Sixth Sense?' he said.

'Yes?'

'This plan of ours is all very well, but haven't we forgotten something rather important?'

'What?' said Sixth Sense.

'Well, I, for one, have absolutely no idea *how* to make this work! Aren't I supposed to chant some magic words or something? I mean, it's not just going to *happen* all by itself, is it?'

'Oh, don't you worry about that!' said Sixth Sense. 'It'll all come naturally. Just wait for my signal, focus on what needs to happen, and you'll be fine.' She hurried on in front. Walter shrugged his shoulders and followed. He had no idea what Sixth Sense meant, but all of a sudden felt a lot more confident.

They soon reached the small bush that stood directly across the street from the Braithwaites' house. Walter ducked down behind it.

It wasn't a bad hiding place, except that the top of his hat was visible from the far side, which made the bush look rather ridiculous.

'Uh-oh, looks like they're arguing!' said Walter.

Peering through the branches he could see the silhouettes of one of the twins struggling over the remote control with his younger brother and the second twin fiddling with the game console.

'I'll check it's the right game,' whispered Sixth Sense. Before Walter could reply Sixth Sense had darted across the road, in through their garden gate and jumped up onto their window ledge.

Looking in she saw the three Braithwaite boys sitting in a row on their sofa (the smallest one puffy-eyed and licking a biscuit) gaping at the start of the *Planet Voss Monster Battle* game. 'Perfect,' she whispered.

At that moment George looked around and spotted her. 'Hey, look, Tom. It's that cute cat again!'

'Oooh! It's *so* cute!' piped up Thomas, jumping up. 'I want a cat like that!'

Sixth Sense dived off the ledge, shot out of the garden and back across the road.

'Bye, bye, Kitty!' called Thomas, waving at the empty window ledge. Then he sat back down between his brothers.

'We're ready, partner,' Sixth Sense said solemnly, rejoining Walter behind the bush. She sat down and gazed deeply into his eyes.

Immediately Walter's mind started to swim and a translucent haze appeared, seeming to separate him from his cat and the rest of his surroundings. Then, not knowing what had taken hold of him, he stood up from behind the bush, and raised his great-grandpa's wand high in the air. Sixth Sense blinked three times, her eyes still fixed on Walter's. 'Let the magic begin!' she said, in an echoing voice that sent a warm shiver down Walter's spine. Walter then heard himself cry out, 'Jeepers creepers! Zabadabadoo!' in a voice that didn't *quite* sound like his own.

Things immediately began to happen. First the silver

tip of the magician's wand began to glow and make a fizz-popping noise, like the sound a can of sparkling drink makes when it's opened. Then, through the fizzing and popping, came Sixth Sense's chanting whisper: 'Focus, Walter, focus.'

Walter stared ahead, eyes locked wide, as he pictured the *Planet Voss* monsters vanishing one by one from the game battle scene. 'Now you see them, now you don't!' he murmured.

'Now you see them, now now you don't—'

Just as he found his rhythm, a loud crack and smashing sound jolted him out of his trance.

'Here we go! Here we go!' cried Sixth Sense. And she began jumping about on the pavement, not unlike a cat on a hot tin roof.

Walter stood calmly staring into the room from across the road. Then, as he saw what he saw, his mouth began to open in slow motion.

5

WARRIORS ON THE LOOSE

Inside the Braithwaites' cinema room all conversation had stopped after Sixth Sense had left the window ledge. Harry, George, and little Thomas Braithwaite all watched in silence as, on the faraway planet of Voss, the Crystal Warrior King of the Iceberg Kingdom (controlled by Harry) prepared to lead his army of White Crystal Warriors into battle against the Flaming Fire Fiends from Volcano Island (commanded by George).

Wide grins appeared on the boys' faces as the Crystal Warrior King bellowed, '**C-r-y-s-t-a-l F-r-e-e- z-e A-t-t-a-c-k!**' signalling the start of the battle.

Harry pressed his controller button. Instantly his White Crystal Warriors snapped into teams of four interlocking ice crystals, each group ready to attack the army of Flaming Fire Fiends, which approached in single file from over the ridge of the iceberg.

'*Ace!*' shouted little Thomas, from between his brothers, as the lead team of White Crystal Warriors hurled itself into the first oncoming Fire Fiend, freezing it into a flame-shaped ice block.

'*Die!*' yelled Harry, jabbing at his controller again as one of his shimmering ice warriors broke free from the formation and plunged itself into the frozen Fire Fiend, just to be sure no flames lingered inside.

'*Revenge!*' bellowed George, purple-faced, as he thumb-punched his controller in a frenzy, already summoning his next Fire Fiend.

'*Go! Go!*' said Thomas, as Harry's next team of White Crystal Warriors lined up ready to take on the second Fire Fiend that was now blasting across the ice towards them.

But then, quite suddenly, something strange happened. Instead of hurling themselves at the second Flaming Fire Fiend, the second team of White Crystal Warriors turned to face Harry, George and Thomas where they were sitting on the sofa.

'***Coming out!***' yelled their team leader, fixing an icy stare through the screen onto Harry. Before Harry could react, the interlocking group of four White Crystal Warriors propelled itself towards the television screen and smashed right through it into the sitting room, sending glass cracking and splintering to the ground.

The breakout had separated the four White Crystal Warriors from their formation and they now paused mid-air, side by side, to shake their loosened frost particles to the carpet.

'O-n-w-a-r-d-s!' commanded the lead warrior in a high voice as he glared at all three boys down his sparkling nose. Then he shot sideways across the room, and up and out of the half-open window with the rest of his team in his wake.

'Woah! What's going on?' cried Harry, staring in bewilderment as he followed the path of the White Crystal Warriors out of the open window.

'They've smashed the TV!' gasped George.

'Awesome!' shouted Thomas, eyes wide as the last warrior disappeared.

A high-pitched whizzing filled the room. Harry, George and Thomas swivelled their heads back towards the smashed TV to find the whole army of White Crystal Warriors — followed up at the rear by the Crystal Warrior King himself — queuing up and propelling themselves out of the hole in the middle of the screen. *Pfum! Pfum! Pfum!* Out they came one after the other, their frosty, glittering eyes filled with panicked excitement. And as each one burst through, it paused mid-air to shake clouds of white frost to the ground before being sucked up across the room sideways and whooshed out of the window.

In less than 30 seconds the Crystal Ice Warriors and their king were gone. A layer of frost covered the carpet and the three boys sat shivering and shocked into a brief silence.

'*The Fire Fiends are coming!*' Thomas, his face bright red, almost launched off the sofa from his sitting position.

All three boys' faces contorted with terror as they stared back at the screen. The Flaming Fire Fiends, who had continued to appear over the ridge of the iceberg, were scrabbling around trying to work out where the enemy had gone when their leader spotted the hole in the television screen. *The Ice Warriors have escaped!'* it bellowed in a breathy roar, pointing at the screen and belching orange, green and red flames. *'O-n-w-a-r-d-s and o-u-t! T-o the m-e-l-t-d-o-w-n!'*

The well-trained army of Flaming Fire Fiends instantly huddled together to form a single multi-headed fireball, then charged at the television screen.

Harry, George and Thomas shrieked and cupped their hands over their faces (leaving just enough space between their fingers to see what was happening) as the ball of flaming heads shot out through the hole, raged across the living room towards them and, in the last split second, zoomed sideways up and out of the window, narrowly avoiding slamming into them.

'Fire! Fire!' shouted Thomas, even though the moment had passed.

'**Argh — what's that?!**' Harry felt something wet and prickly starting to attack his feet. He looked down. The heat thrown out by the fireball had melted the white carpet of frost left by the White Crystal Warriors, leaving pools of water mixed with shattered glass, which was now seeping into his socks.

George looked down and raised his own dripping feet from the soaked rug beneath him. 'Ugh! This sucks!'

Footsteps thumped along the hallway.

'Uh, oh!' said Harry.

'Oh dear!' said George.

The door flung open.

'What on *earth* is going on?!' Mrs Braithwaite's voice was so high it seemed to squeeze out from the top of her throat.

A brief silence filled the room as she stared, aghast, at the shattered television screen and three agitated boys all red in the face.

'It blew up!' said Harry.

'By itself!' added George, flicking Harry a stern sideways glance. (She'd never believe the truth.)

Harry nodded in agreement, quickly putting on the blank stare he always used when telling half-truths.

'The monsters broke it!' said Thomas, in his helpful voice.

The twins groaned and rolled their eyes, knowing that a bad situation had just got a whole lot worse.

'This glass is lethal, boys! **Outside, now!**' Mrs Braithwaite's cheeks had turned as red as traffic lights, which everyone knew was not a good sign. (It usually only happened when she couldn't remember her lines.) 'And I suggest you get your story straight on what *really* happened — Dad's back in half an hour and we'll need an explanation!'

Thomas skipped past their mother out of the room.

Harry and George followed, their cheeks now white, each trying to think of how to explain away the smashed TV.

The time that passed between the first White Crystal Warrior turning to stare out of the television set at Harry, and the multi-headed fireball monster finally disappearing out of the window was no more than a minute, although it seemed a lot longer to everyone involved. During this time, Walter had stood across the road with his eyes and mouth expanding into ever larger circles.

Finally, when he saw the White Crystal Warriors zooming up towards the window and heading in his direction, he'd had enough. 'This is too much, Sixth Sense! Make it stop!' he shouted. With that, Walter ceremoniously lifted his top hat from his head (about ten centimetres), in the hope that everything would return to normal.

'Put it back! Put it back on!' cried Sixth Sense, but Walter, of course, couldn't hear her.

The White Crystal Warriors were still streaking in Walter's direction.

'Into the hat! Into the hat! Regroup!' commanded the

Crystal Warrior King from the rear. (With his crystal clear vision, he could spot a safe haven at any distance.)

Before Walter had time to blink, the whole army of White Crystal Warriors had skimmed over the top of his head and gone whistling high up inside his top hat, leaving his eyebrows dusted with frost.

In panic, Walter snapped the magician's hat hard onto his head.

'The Fire Fiends, get the Fire Fiends!' shouted Sixth Sense.

Feeling the approaching heat, Walter looked up to see the multi-headed fireball monster hurtling towards him. Obediently he whisked off the hat and in it zoomed, melting the frost on his eyebrows as it went. Then, *snap!* Down came the hat again onto Walter Brown's head.

Silence followed as Sixth Sense sat trembling with excitement, staring up at Walter. Then, slowly building up from inside the hat, came a hissing, fizzing and bubbling noise. This was quickly followed by dense jets of steam that spurted from under the brim, giving Walter the appearance of a magician whose trick had just spectacularly backfired.

Walter groaned. His head and hair were soaked, and very quickly warm water started pouring from inside the hat down his face, over the tips of his ears and down the back of his neck.

'Brilliant!' cried Sixth Sense. 'They've extinguished each other! Now *that* is clever magic!'

'Clever?' cried Walter. 'Just look at me, will you? My head feels disgusting!'

Sixth Sense's fur suddenly stood on end. 'The twins are about to come out,' she whispered.

'What? There's *no way* I want to meet them now!' said Walter, glaring. 'Let's get out of here...'

Walter and Sixth Sense dashed back down the road and were out of sight just before the boys opened their front door.

6

THE DUEL

'What's happened to you?' said Hannah as Walter, still dripping water, burst through the kitchen back door.

Sixth Sense whisked in at his ankles, her tail set unusually low.

'Oh, er... just some kids messing about with a hose down the road,' said Walter, trying to catch his breath.

Hannah frowned, and tried to sound important. 'Mum and Dad have gone to set up the party for later. You'd better go and get cleaned up before they get back.' Without waiting for his answer she picked up her pen and carried on with her Viking project, which was spread out over the kitchen table.

'Okay, okay,' said Walter wearily. 'It is my birthday, you know, Han. You don't need to be quite so grumpy!' Walter loved his big sister, but since she'd turned 13 she'd become a bit too serious, not to mention hard to predict. Whenever she was left in charge she chopped and changed between acting like a grown-up (and being really boring) and going back to her old self (and being good fun), depending on what was going on.

'By the way,' she said (suddenly forgetting to sound important), 'I'm still only half way through my homework, so I guess your first spell didn't work, eh? Ha! Ha!'

But Walter couldn't reply. Instead he snapped his eyes shut and started shaking his head hard from side to side. Something inside his hat wasn't quite right.

'Quick!' shouted Sixth Sense, bolting towards the hallway door, her fur bristling. 'You need to get out of here!'

Walter ignored Sixth Sense. He was getting more and more agitated as what felt like frozen pinpricks started to dance around on top of his head.

'*Oww!*' he screeched, staring at Hannah and pulling the top hat tightly at the brim. Now something that felt like a red-hot poker was jumping about on top of his head, in between the frozen pinpricks.

'What *is* the matter?' said Hannah, as Walter began to shake his head again. 'Have you got water in your ears?'

But Walter didn't answer. Instead his eyes froze open in panic as he realised what was happening. The lead warriors in the *Plant Voss* game must have come back to life to fight the Dance of Death. He'd seen it in the adverts. It was a last chance for the loser to earn extra points — and honour — after the main battle. That meant they were duelling on top of his head!

Walter took an inward gasp and made a dash for the hallway door. '*Oww!* Ah! I must get these wet clothes off. *Yow!* That's *sore!*' He raced up the stairs, closely followed by Sixth Sense and slammed his bedroom door.

Back in the kitchen Hannah shook her head and rolled her eyes. 'Boys…' she said with a sigh, then carried on with her note taking.

Once safely inside his bedroom Walter ripped the top hat from his head and threw it towards his desk.

As it twirled across the room, and just before it knocked over his lamp and fell to the floor out of sight, two tiny figures went flying through the air.

The first, a tiny gesticulating ball of fire made up of a flaming head, and flaming arms and legs, bounced across the floor and disappeared under his bed.

The second, a shimmering shape of ice — and none other than the Crystal Warrior King himself — landed in the middle of the carpet.

Walter stalled and gazed open-mouthed at the ice figure. Sixth Sense leapt onto the bed and stared down, her green eyes glinting.

The Crystal Warrior King stood about ten centimetres tall. His arms, legs and body were made up of what looked like tightly packed icicles. Large frost particles coated his bushy eyebrows and moustache, and his beard looked like a tiny frozen waterfall.

On top of his head the Crystal Warrior King wore what looked like a glass crown but which was, of course, made of ice. And as he frantically turned his head from left to right and back again, trying to see where the Flaming Fire Fiend had disappeared to, his flowing frost-covered hair sparkled like millions of tiny diamonds.

Sixth Sense cocked her head to one side and pricked her fluffy ears forward. *'N-N-N-ice crown!'* she joked, unheard by Walter.

'Less of the chat, cat!' snapped the Crystal Warrior King. 'Where's it gone? Where's it gone?'

The Crystal Warrior King carried on twisting his

head from left to right. 'Come out so I can f-r-e-e-z-e your flames!' he screeched in a high pitch.

'You'll have to come and g-e-t me *Sssp-a-r-kle Face!*' came an echoing cackle from under Walter's bed.

'Show yourself, *Flame-faced Coward!*' roared the Crystal Warrior King (insofar as he could with his high-pitched frosty voice). He waved his glittering dagger icicle arms in the direction of Walter's bed, and started lunging back and forth.

Walter, who couldn't hear any of this without his hat, chuckled as he watched the ice king trying to coax out his enemy.

'Go on! Go after it!' he shouted eagerly, unaware that the Fire Fiend's glow underneath his bed was rapidly growing in size.

Sixth Sense, whose bottom was beginning to feel more than a little warm, began leaping around, trying to get Walter's attention.

'The bed, the bed!' she shouted. 'It'll all go up in flames — get the hat on, Walter! We've got to get the Fire Fiend out!'

The Flaming Fire Fiend was now breathing stronger and stronger flame jets, which eventually slithered into sight, like orange serpent tongues, as it tried to reach the White Crystal Warrior King.

On seeing the flames, Walter shrieked and grabbed a towel from the radiator, then dived onto the carpet to try to smother them, but missed. Instead he found himself eyeball-to-eyeball with the Flaming Fire Fiend as it hovered just out of reach.

In the same moment, Sixth Sense, who could no longer stand the heat, leapt off the bed.

This had an unexpected effect. The Flaming Fire Fiend, faced with the glinting green eyes of a giant fluffy monster alongside Walter's, took a sharp inward gasp and drew in its flames.

'*Whha....is that?*' it breathed in a tiny roar, fear flickering in its eyes for the first time in its battle-hardened gaming life. It then propelled itself in a fireball along the floor towards the head of the bed and sizzled along the bottom of the wall to the other side of the room.

Walter jumped up to find the Fire Fiend hovering by the radiator under his window, dangerously close to his curtains. Butterflies flew in frenzied circles in his tummy. He flicked a glance towards his desk, but his hat was out of reach on the floor. Should he try to extinguish the Flaming Fire Fiend without Sixth Sense's help, or leave it to the ice king? He gripped his wand with his right hand, but hesitated. He couldn't risk experimenting with magic and fire — not after the mess he'd made of his first spell.

Sixth Sense arched her back and hissed menacingly in the Fire Fiend's direction and it dimmed its flames again.

Seizing his chance, Walter dashed across the room and scooped up his hat from under his desk.

'Leave it! Leave it! He's mine!' he heard the Crystal Warrior King screeching as he pulled his hat on.

'Stay back! Stay back!' Sixth Sense cried in reply, knowing that the combined heat of the radiator and the Fire Fiend would be the little king's undoing. But it was too late. The White Crystal Warrior King let out a chilling scream and charged to certain meltdown.

The Fire Fiend's flames doubled in size as they

engulfed the tiny ice king and were now licking towards the edge of the curtains.

'*Stop!*' Walter bellowed, his whole body shaking.

'At last!' called Sixth Sense, seeing the hat on his head.

And as she turned and looked into his eyes, Walter's wand was already raised high in the air.

7

FOUND OUT

Walter felt the familiar warm shiver down his spine as he looked deep into Sixth Sense's green eyes. 'Focus,' he heard her chant, and very quickly the room began to dissolve into the background.

Walter's wand began to fizz, pop and glow, as before. Once again, he heard himself starting to cry, 'Jeepers creepers!' in a voice that didn't sound *quite* like his own.

'What's going on up there, Walter?' Hannah's grown-up voice echoed up the stairs.

Clump, clump, clump. Her footsteps were now fast approaching.

The haze around Walter began fading in and out as he tried in vain to visualise the Fire Fiend shrivelling up and disappearing. He lost concentration and stalled mid-chant.

'Get on with it! Get on with it!' cried Sixth Sense, but Walter could no longer focus. He froze in panic and dropped his wand. The room came back into clear view and he saw the Flaming Fire Fiend drawing in its flames as the last drops of the Crystal Warrior King evaporated.

Hannah flung open Walter's bedroom door just as Sixth Sense leapt back onto the bed and the Fire Fiend sizzled up behind the radiator.

'What was all that noise, Walter?' she demanded. 'And who were you shouting "Stop" at?' She paused, staring at the carpet.

'Walter, *what* are all those burn marks?'

Walter shook his head and faltered, looking across for support to Sixth Sense, who lay nonchalantly on the bed, washing herself and looking every inch a normal cat. 'Nothing! No one...' he said, and then added sternly, 'I mean, it was just our *clumsy cat* knocking over my lamp again!'

Sixth Sense looked up indignantly but on seeing Walter's cold glare decided not to answer back.

Walter held his breath, praying that Hannah would believe him.

'Well,' said Hannah, 'Mum and Dad will be back soon, so you'd better get yourself sorted out quickly.' As she turned to leave she glanced towards the radiator, which Walter kept eyeing nervously. 'What *are* you looking at over there?' she said.

'Nothing,' said Walter, lying.

Hannah frowned, then started marching towards the radiator.

Sixth Sense sat up. '*Uh-oh!*' she muttered in a resigned voice.

Hannah got to within two steps of the radiator when the Flaming Fire Fiend burst out from behind it, shot across the carpet between her feet and out of the bedroom door. A black, smouldering scorch line followed in its wake.

'After it!' cried Sixth Sense, leaping from the bed.

Hannah stood briefly stunned as her young brother

and his cat streaked out of the door in hot pursuit of the bizarre fiery ball.

'Wait for me!' she suddenly cried, eyes alight. Walter was clearly involved in something awesome of which she wanted to be a part. With all ideas of responsibility and growing up abandoned, she thundered down the stairs after him.

8

FINAL FREEZE

'Where's it gone?' shouted Hannah, flying off the bottom stair and looking left and right.

'It's in here!' called Walter from the kitchen, relieved to have his sister onside.

Hannah raced through the doorway to see the tiny Fire Fiend dancing madly on top of the stainless steel bread bin above its upside-down reflection.

Sixth Sense jumped up onto the kitchen counter beside the bread bin and arched her back, hissing in the monster's direction. The Fire Fiend fixed its glowing red eyes on her, but didn't budge from its vantage point.

'What *is* that thing?' gasped Hannah.

'It's from the Braithwaite twins' *Planet Voss* game. I'll explain later!' said Walter breathlessly.

'You *what*?' Hannah frowned deeply. This was clearly

some kind of clever prank. She scratched the underside of her chin. Then it clicked — Walter's chemistry set! This was a failed experiment that had got out of hand. What's more, *she* was the butt of the joke. She folded her arms and leaned against the refrigerator, shaking her head. 'Very funny, Walter!'

'I'm not joking!' said Walter, his eyes widening in panic as scorch marks began creeping up the wall behind the Fire Fiend. The whole house could go up in flames at any minute.

'Time for magic,' he breathed.

But as he jerked his right hand forward, he found himself gripping thin air. His stomach lurched as he pictured the wand falling from his hands upstairs.

Magic was out of the question.

Walter glanced desperately around the kitchen, searching for ideas. He looked back in despair back at Hannah — then his eyes rested on the refrigerator behind her. 'Sixth Sense — the freezer. Let's try to get it in the freezer!'

'Brilliant!' shouted Sixth Sense, her eyes still on the Fire Fiend.

'*Sixth Sense?* What *are* you talking about?' said Hannah.

'Quick, Hannah!' shouted Walter. 'Open the freezer door. I'll try to scare it in!'

At that moment the Fire Fiend threw its arms up and let out a breathy cackle, then hurled itself from the bread bin, over Sixth Sense's head, and onto the kitchen table — landing just a few centimetres from Hannah's homework.

'Get it off there, Walter!'

Hannah stared in horror as the Fire Fiend began breathing flames in the direction of her Viking project papers. 'If your bonkers fireball experiment ruins my project I'll never speak to you again!'

Sixth Sense leapt across to the table and positioned herself squarely on top of Hannah's homework, growling and arching her back. The wooden tabletop started to smoke and turn black beneath the Fire Fiend's tiny dancing feet.

'Open the freezer door!' yelled Walter again. The pitch and frenzy in Walter's voice finally jerked Hannah into action and she stepped forward and pulled open the freezer door.

'Quick! Get your wand!' shouted Sixth Sense. 'I'll hold it here.'

'On it!' Walter turned and raced out of the door.

'*You what?* Walter, come back!' called Hannah, still staring at the dancing fire creature. And the more she stared, the more she wondered whether perhaps it wasn't a joke after all.

Walter reappeared, breathless, wand in hand, just as the Fire Fiend swivelled round and breathed a mammoth flame right across the room and onto the window blind above the sink. As the blind burst into flames, Hannah let out a shriek and dashed towards the kitchen tap. But already the Fire Fiend was looking around for other targets.

Sixth Sense continued to spit and scowl, trying to distract the Fire Fiend. Walter knew he had to act without her help this time — and he had to make this work. He breathed in deeply through his nose, immediately dismissing the tingle in his tummy. 'Focus,' he whispered to himself, remembering what Great-grandpa Horace had said. 'Focus!' he repeated.

A quiet calm took hold of him as he reached deep inside, drawing on all his powers of concentration. Then a familiar warm shiver ran down his spine as he raised his wand ceremoniously into the air. He felt confident, bold, strong. And now, with his gaze fixed on the tiny raging monster, he conjured up a clear image of the Fire Fiend being sucked across the room and into the freezer, while the flames on the kitchen blind extinguished.

He was just *starting* to cry 'Jeepers creepers!' (in a voice that didn't sound *quite* like his own) when the Fire Fiend jerked its head right and saw him in the doorway. Instantly its flames dimmed to green and blue, and it launched itself into the air, where it paused, twisting, writhing and cackling above the kitchen table.

'Zabadabadoo!' boomed Walter, and swished his wand down through the air. The Fire Fiend went limp and let out a piercing scream. It then shot sideways across the room and in through the open freezer door.

Hannah raced to the freezer and slammed the door shut. 'Got it!' she shouted. A muffled hissing and fizzing came from inside it. Then silence.

Walter looked towards the kitchen window — the fire was out. 'Awesome!' he said breathlessly, then punched the air and offered up a high five to his sister.

Hannah started to raise her hand, but then changed her mind. Instead she sat down at the table, locked her eyebrows in a deep V and assumed her grown-up voice.

'Okay. So what's going on, Walter? You'd better explain now — you're going to be in such trouble when Mum and Dad get back.'

Walter darted a sideways glance at Sixth Sense, looking for help — but she had her mind on other things. 'Cripes!' he said, following her gaze as she crouched on the floor, ears pricked forward. Water was streaming out from under the freezer door.

'Uh-oh!' said Sixth Sense. She sat bolt upright, twitching her tail from side to side. 'They're on their way. Sorry, Walter, got distracted.'

'Who?' said Walter.

'Pardon?' said Hannah.

'Your parents!' said Sixth Sense. '*Correction* — they're here!'

Tyres crunched across the gravel in the driveway, accompanied by the low rumble of a car engine.

The water was now gushing across the floor and had started to form a small lake on the far side of the room. Walter's cheeks turned numb as he looked all around — at the flood, the scorched table and walls, the blackened blinds — and as he pictured the devastation in his bedroom. He had to fix it all — and fast. He'd worry about Hannah later. There was no time to explain.

He took a deep breath and focused deep inside once

again, picturing the kitchen and his bedroom and the stair carpet exactly as they had been before.

Immediately a warm shiver ran down his spine and he raised his wand ceremoniously into the air.

Car doors slammed outside, but Walter stayed focused.

'Jeepers creepers! Zabadabadoo!' he cried confidently, in a voice that didn't sound *quite* like his own.

'What the—?' Hannah stared saucer-eyed at the now glowing, fizzing and popping wand. A blinding flash filled the kitchen. Something seemed to shudder. Walter looked up — the scorch marks on the wall and table were gone and the blind hung intact at the kitchen window. He looked down — the kitchen floor was bone dry.

'It worked!' cried Walter, casting his eyes around for approval. Even his hat and clothes were dry.

'Bravo, partner — all clear upstairs!' Sixth Sense appeared through the kitchen doorway.

Walter heard his parents' voices in the driveway.

'What? What's worked?' said Hannah, suddenly shaking her head and frowning. '*Hang on!*' she said, looking all around. 'When did you creep in here? Did I just fall asleep doing my homework?'

Walter clapped his hand to his mouth. Had he

accidentally *wiped his sister's memory* when putting everything back to how it had been? Was that awesome, or freaky? He couldn't decide. Either way, it solved one huge problem. 'Er… must have…' he said. He paused, then pulled a goofy cross-eyed face at her. 'Getting some beauty sleep before my birthday party, I bet!'

Hannah sighed and glanced at the ceiling, then crossed her eyes at him. 'They're all three years younger than me, Walter! *Duh!*'

Walter backed into the hallway, giving his sister a wide silly grin. He then turned and zipped up the stairs just before the keys turned in the front door.

'Well, partner,' said Sixth Sense as Walter closed his bedroom door. 'I knew we'd have some close shaves today, but not quite *that* close! You did splendidly, if I may say so.' She lowered her head and started licking her chest.

Walter took a deep, faltering breath. Shock and anger were quickly setting in and he felt his body start to tremble. 'Splendidly?' he said slowly, in a cross, low voice. 'Sixth Sense, do you realise the whole house nearly went up in flames just now? We could have all died!'

Sixth Sense studied the floor but said nothing.

'What's more,' Walter went on, his voice now shaking, 'not only did I NOT MEET the twins, I also managed to break their television AND their *Planet Voss* game, AND they'll get the blame! They'll never speak to me if they find out it was me!'

Sixth Sense stayed silent. She seemed to be concentrating on something.

Walter laid his wand carefully on the bed. 'Look, don't get me wrong, Sixth Sense,' he said, trying not to sound so cross this time. 'This magic thing's really awesome, but it's also really dangerous — you saw the mess I made.'

Sixth Sense mumbled to herself and began licking her left paw.

'In fact,' said Walter, now irritated by her silence, 'the more I think about it, the more I think I should just put Great-grandpa Horace's hat and wand back in their box and forget all about them.'

'*Forget?*' said Sixth Sense, dropping her paw. 'Don't be ridiculous, Walter. You can't forget! You took your magic to a new level just now — and without my help. You can do it!'

Walter didn't reply.

'What's more,' she added, 'I think you'll soon find

there are *other* things you can do that you didn't think were possible when you woke up this morning.'

'Pardon?' said Walter. Why did Sixth Sense always have to talk in riddles?

'Look, I'm sorry you didn't get to meet the twins,' she said. 'And about the smashed TV — I guess we just forgot to focus on *how* the monsters would escape.' She glanced at the ceiling with a brief look of regret. '*Devil's in the detail...* But you did brilliantly in the end, Walter. And I'll make everything up to you, I promise.'

She stood up and began parading around the room, ignoring his silence. 'Anyway, remember, your great-grandpa chose us for a reason — you can't just give up like that.'

Walter sat down on the side of his bed and chewed his bottom lip. His thoughts tumbled one over the other.

He was still furious with Sixth Sense for the failed experiment, and for the danger it had put everyone in, but it was, he supposed, her first time testing the magic too, and something deep down told him he could trust her. Besides, after his disastrous start hadn't he managed to perform magic on his own that really worked — not once, but twice? And if Great-grandpa Horace had chosen them for a reason, perhaps he should take Sixth Sense's advice?

'Okay, okay,' he said with a sigh. 'I won't banish the

hat for now — but no more smashing up people's things!'

'Deal!' said Sixth Sense, flashing her eyes at him.

She shook her head, sat down and stared into the space in front of her. 'Oooh...!'

'*What?*' said Walter as Sixth Sense's eyes started to glaze over.

'I've just seen something... Oh! How very interesting...'

'*What, Sixth Sense?*'

'Well...' she said dreamily, seeming to look at and through Walter at the same time, 'I think it might be where we're going abroad. I can see mountains... and... snow...and — ah — *Oh no*...it's fading!'

She stood up and shook herself out. 'Sorry, partner. It's gone. Looks like we'll just have to wait and see.'

'When? How soon?' asked Walter, a mixture of curiosity and dread taking hold. 'I'm really not sure I'm ready for this—'

'No need to fret,' said Sixth Sense. 'It won't be for a good while yet. Relax!'

Walter let out a breath. 'Phew! Well, thank goodness for that!' He sat down on his bed and slipped off his gloves. 'Now, I hope you don't mind, Sixth Sense, but we're having an early lunch today. Then I have my football birthday party to get ready for.'

'So you do!' said Sixth Sense. 'Oh, I nearly forgot — Happy birthday, Walter!'

Walter grinned at his cat, then plucked his top hat from his head and twirled it across his room, where (this time) it landed neatly on his desk.

9

ANOTHER BIRTHDAY SURPRISE

A large plate of peanut butter and jam sandwiches sat in the middle of the table. 'Thanks, Dad,' said Walter as everyone sat down. 'These look yummy!'

In Walter's opinion, his dad made the best peanut butter and jam sandwiches and he'd made a special request for them today.

'Happy birthday, Walter!' said his dad. 'Go easy though — you've got your party food later.'

'Happy birthday, bigger little brother,' said Hannah with a wide grin. 'You'll never catch me up!'

'Happy birthday!' said his mum, passing the plate around.

Everyone reached for a sandwich and Walter rolled his eyes as the delicious mix of soft bread, peanut butter and jam oozed and melted in his mouth with his first bite.

'Ugh! That's disgusting!' said Hannah through a muffled chew. Her head was bowed as she stared into her lap.

'What is?' said her mum. 'I thought you liked peanut butter?'

Hannah lifted up *Vikings: Everything You Ever Wanted To Know,'* with a cheeky grin.

'Hannah, I've told you — no books at the table!' said Mrs Brown.

'I think they gave this the wrong title,' said Hannah. 'It should be *Vikings: Everything You **Don't Want To Know.'***

'Ha! Ha! Hannah the Viking hater!' said Walter, and bit with relish into his second sandwich.

'By the way, Walter, have you met the twins up the road yet?' said his dad.

'Er...no... Why?' Walter's heart skipped a beat.

'No reason — was just wondering when we passed their house earlier.'

'Their parents were throwing out a huge TV with a smashed screen,' said Walter's mum, reaching for the water jug. 'It looked brand new. I wonder if it fell off the wall?'

'Not the one Walter and Todd were spying on the other week?' said Hannah, laughing.

'No we didn't!' said Walter, in a high voice. He continued chewing but all of a sudden his sandwich had no taste. His heart sank and his cheeks began to burn as he stared down at his plate.

It was his own stupid fault that the twins' brand new TV was smashed. They were bound to get the blame and he'd never be able to look them in the eye, no matter what Sixth Sense had promised. So much for making new friends.

His tummy began to ache and he suddenly wished it wasn't his birthday after all.

At that moment the doorbell rang.

'I'll get it,' said Hannah, jumping up. 'More birthday presents, I bet, Walter.'

But he didn't look up. He didn't want any more presents.

Voices filled the hallway.

'Sixpence, you naughty girl,' Walter heard Hannah saying. 'She belongs to my brother.'

Hannah marched into the kitchen with Sixth Sense in her arms. Harry, George and Thomas Braithwaite followed right behind.

Walter's eyes jumped wide as he gulped on his mouthful of sandwich.

'This is Harry, George and Thomas,' said Hannah.

'Hi, boys! Nice to meet you,' said Walter's mum.

His dad got up and shook their hands.

'Hi!' they said.

'This is my brother, Walter. He owns Sixpence,' said Hannah, pointing. 'Oh — and it's his birthday today, by the way.'

'Hi, Walter. Happy birthday!' said Harry quickly.

'Many happy returns!' said George with a wide smile.

Thomas seemed to be hiding behind them.

'Hi there,' said Walter. He swallowed hard, wishing he could think of something cool to say but his mind had blanked.

'We're really sorry,' said George, 'but our little brother loves your cat so much he took her in — we found him playing with her in his bedroom.'

'We let her out but she kept coming back,' said Harry. 'So we figured we'd better find out where she lives and bring her home.'

'Actually, we were pleased she lives here — we've been planning to come and say hi since we moved in,' said George. 'It's quite hard meeting new friends in the holidays.'

Walter found himself smiling inside.

Thomas, who'd been hiding behind Harry's legs, poked his head out and grinned, then bent down to stroke Sixth Sense as Hannah placed her on the kitchen floor.

'That's so kind of you, boys,' said Mrs Brown.

'No bother at all,' said George. 'She kind of saved the day after our TV broke this morning. Thomas was really fed up so I think she took his mind off it. He's found moving house a bit confusing.'

'We saw the TV earlier — it certainly looked very broken,' said Mrs Brown. 'I hope no one was hurt. Did it fall?'

Walter felt his cheeks flush. He took a deep inward breath.

'It blew up!' said Harry quickly, then glanced at his twin.

George started to blush. 'Yes, it did, er, kind of...'

'Boom!' shouted Thomas, suddenly jumping up. 'Then all the monsters came out!'

'Ha! Ha!' said Hannah. 'And did you fight them?'

Walter continued holding his breath.

Thomas shook his head. 'They escaped through the window...'

'Tom sometimes thinks the games are for real,' said George, ruffling his little brother's hair and staring awkwardly at the space between Walter and Mrs Brown. 'Dad said it must have been a fault inside the telly because of the way the glass blew outwards — the shop said we can change it.'

'Mum thought we'd done it to start with,' said Harry, rolling his eyes.

Walter breathed out as a wave of relief washed over him. 'That happened to a friend's cousin once,' he said in his best casual voice. He crossed his fingers under the table to make up for his white lie.

'Good to hear no one was hurt,' said Mrs Brown.

'No, just a bit of glass in our socks!' said Harry, grinning.

'Well, we'd better go. It was nice to meet you,' said

George. As they turned to leave he spotted Walter's Northern Lights book on the side. 'Hey, cool book! I love astronomy. Is that yours, Walter?'

'Yup,' said Walter, beaming. 'My best friend Todd gave it to me for my birthday.'

He hesitated, but only for a moment. 'Actually, I'm having a football party later — do you all want to come?' He glanced at his parents who smiled and nodded. 'It's at 3.30 over at the sports centre.'

'Awesome!' said George and Harry together.

'Thomas doesn't like playing,' said George, as he watched his little brother follow Sixth Sense into the hall. 'But he enjoys watching.'

'And I like birthday cake!' called Thomas.

'And you've got good hearing!' Hannah called back, with a laugh.

'Well, that's great,' said Walter's mum, reaching for a pen and piece of paper. 'Here's our number — if you ask your mum or dad to call us, we'll confirm the details with them.'

'Cool!' said Harry. He waved the piece of paper in the air. 'Thanks, Walter. See you later!'

'Great!' said Walter, smiling.

'See you later!' said George.

'I'll see you out,' said Walter's dad.

'Bye bye, Sixpence!' they heard Thomas saying out in the hallway.

As the front door slammed, Hannah started frowning and scratching under her chin.

'What's up, Han?' said Mr Brown as he walked back into the kitchen.

She frowned some more. 'Just something about Thomas's escaping monsters story seemed familiar — must have been a TV programme I saw.'

'I think I saw that one too!' said Walter quickly. 'I think we saw it together.' He smiled and double-crossed his fingers under the table.

'Yeah, I guess,' said Hannah, pouring herself a glass of water.

Walter cleared his throat, uncrossed his fingers and reached for his third sandwich. He took a huge bite. Great-grandpa Horace was right — ten was a magical age, and in more ways than one. This was turning out to be a great birthday after all — and who knew what adventures lay ahead? (Well, apart from Sixth Sense, he supposed.)

At that moment a tall fluffy black tail paraded into the kitchen. Sixth Sense paused for a few licks of water from her bowl, then stepped into her basket.

Walter looked across with a grin and winked at her.

Sixth Sense, appearing not to notice, delivered a cavernous yawn, then curled onto her side and fell into a deep, satisfied sleep.

The End (for now...)

WRITE A REVIEW AND GET A FREE POSTER!

KAREN WOULD LOVE TO HEAR WHAT YOU THINK!

If you enjoyed Walter Brown and the Magician's Hat, it would be **magical** if you could leave a review on your preferred bookstore website. Ask a grown-up to show you how. It will help other children and parents find Walter's story :-) If a grown-up emails Karen a link to your review at kpinglis@wellsaidpress.com she will write back to you **and** send a link to free Walter posters!

WALTER BROWN'S NEXT ADVENTURE

To be the first to know when the next Walter book is out visit **kareninglisauthor.com** and sign up to Karen's Readers' Club. (We will never share your email address and you'll hear about offers and more free stuff!)

Meet Karen and her other books overleaf...

ABOUT THE AUTHOR

Karen Inglis lives in London, UK. She has two sons who inspired her to write for children. Karen also writes for business but far prefers making up stories :-) She loves reading, daydreaming, music, theatre — oh, and tea!

ALSO BY KAREN INGLIS

The Secret Lake (8-11 yrs)
Eeek! The Runaway Alien (7-10 yrs)
Henry Haynes and the Great Escape (6-8 yrs)
Ferdinand Fox's Big Sleep (3-5 yrs)

Turn the pages to find out more — and to **read the first two chapters of *Eeek! The Runaway Alien* and *The Secret Lake!***

EEEK! THE RUNAWAY ALIEN

A MATCH MADE IN HEAVEN FOR SOCCER FANS AGED 7-10!

Eleven-year-old Charlie can't believe his luck when he opens his door to an alien one morning — a soccer-mad alien who has run away to Earth for the World Cup! Charlie hides Eeek! in his bedroom and only tells his best friend Jake. All is going well until slimy, sci-fi mad Sid Spiker spots Eeek! through his telescope...

"**Laugh out loud funny!**" ~ *LoveReading4Kids*

A firm favourite at schools visits :)
Order from your local bookshop or online

Read Chapters 1 & 2 at the end of this book

THE SECRET LAKE

A PAGE-TURNING TIME TRAVEL ADVENTURE FOR AGES 8-11

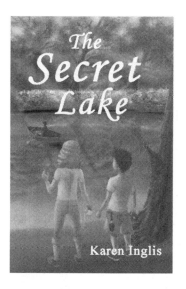

A lost dog, a hidden time tunnel and a secret lake take Stella and Tom to their home and the children living there 100 years in the past. Here they make both friends and enemies, and uncover startling connections with the present...

Enjoyed by over 7,000 readers ~ Search 5-Star reviews

"... an absorbing tale of mystery and suspense" ~ Louise Jordan, The Writers' Advice Centre for Children's Books, London, UK

Order from your local bookshop or online
*Read Chapters 1 & 2 at the end of this book *

HENRY HAYNES AND THE GREAT ESCAPE

A BOY, A BOSSY BOA CONSTRICTOR AND A MAGIC BOOK — OH,
AND A VERY SMELLY GORILLA! (FOR AGES 6-8)

When Henry complains that his new library book is boring he gets sucked down inside and forced to help Brian, a bossy boa, and Gordon (a VERY smelly gorilla) with their zoo escape plan. Can Henry get home alive? And why didn't he keep his big mouth shut about boring stories?!

"... zips along with customary fizz and verve...both exciting and funny in equal measure. "Louise Jordan, The Writers' Advice Centre for Children's Books

Take care not to fall in!

Order from your local bookshop or online

FERDINAND FOX'S BIG SLEEP

A DELIGHTFUL RHYMING PICTURE BOOK ABOUT A FOX THAT ONCE FELL ASLEEP IN THE AUTHOR'S GARDEN (3-5 YRS)

" "Ferdinand Fox curled up in the sun, as the church of St Mary struck quarter past one. His tummy was full, he was ready for sleep, and closing his eyes he began to count sheep…"

Read 5-Star reviews online
Also available as a colouring book or story app
Order from your local bookshop or online

Eeek!
The runaway alien

KAREN INGLIS

ONE

It was a fairly typical Saturday morning in our house. Dad was in the garden emptying out the shed (again!). Mum had gone to the gym for her early morning workout. Rory (my four-year-old brother) was on the sofa wearing Dad's snorkel and mask watching his favourite underwater scene in 'Finding Nemo'. I was scoring goals against the kitchen wall in front of an imaginary crowd of 50,000.

That's when the doorbell rang.

'I'll get it!' I shouted. I don't know why I shouted, because I knew that neither Dad nor Rory could hear me. As I rushed down the hall to open the front door I tried to guess which of the following it would be:

1. Little Joe Williams from next door asking for his football back (yet again!)

2. Someone selling tea towels

3. Our postman with a parcel

4. The National Lottery man to say we'd won (dream on!)

or

5. Mum, hot and sweaty after the gym, having forgotten her key as usual.

In fact it was none of these. Standing at our door that Saturday morning was, I'm not kidding you, an *alien!*

Now, most people would jump out of their skins at the sight on their doorstep of a bald-headed fluorescent green monster with pale blue smoke wafting from its tiny semicircular ears. But there was something about this alien that touched my heart. Whether it was his large slow-blinking pink-red eyes, his snub nose, his friendly smile, or simply the fact that he was exactly my height, I cannot tell you, but for some reason I just stood there and gawped at him in wonder.

My gawping, and the alien's blinking and smiling, carried on for a good thirty seconds. It was as if I had met a long lost friend and here we were bonding again. But then I nearly jumped out of my skin as an eerie wheezing and rasping noise floated up from behind my right shoulder.

The alien suddenly stopped blinking and pulled such a terrified face as he stared beyond me I was convinced that an enemy being from the far side of Mercury must have zapped down into my house to do battle with him. I swung round in fear for my life — to find Rory, complete with snorkel and mask, staring wide-eyed through his steamed-up visor at our visitor.

The alien couldn't handle the sight of Rory. I think it was the batman outfit that finished him off. Without warning he emitted a strange high-pitched echoing sound, then turned and fled out through our gate and off down the road.

'You idiot, Rory!' I shouted. Rory wheezed through his snorkel, then shrugged his shoulders and held up both hands as if to say, 'What did I do?' Then he disappeared back to his 'Finding Nemo' DVD, whisking his cape behind him like a matador with attitude.

'Well,' I thought to myself, 'I've got two choices here. Either I close the door and pretend this never happened, *or* I race down the road to see if I can find the alien and bring him back.' No prizes for guessing which of these two options I picked.

By the time I got to the gate my fluorescent green friend had almost reached the end of our road.

'Come back!' I called in a feeble voice, knowing he wouldn't hear me.

Just at that moment an almighty roar filled the

morning sky. I looked up to see the Red Arrows streak out through the white-grey clouds, and cut a cool formation right over the top of the houses at the end of the road. Awesome! When I glanced to the end of the road again, the alien had stopped and was jumping up and down in a frenzy, pointing at the planes.

'Poor soul!' I said to myself. 'Probably thinks it's his spaceship come to rescue him.' It would take more than a puff of blue ear-smoke to get him a ride on one of those! And they definitely wouldn't be taking him home — to the government laboratories more likely!

As their last echo faded across the sky the alien, who had calmed down, didn't, as I thought he would, shoot off around the corner. Instead he stood there gazing dreamily into the sky, as if he'd just seen Father Christmas and his reindeers, or a few stray angels.

'An alien trance!' I thought as I started walking towards him. At that moment (had he heard my thoughts?) he switched his gaze out of the sky and down the road towards me. Immediately he started waving vigorously. As I approached I could see a broad grin on his moon-shaped face. He seemed to have found his long-lost soul mate again.

'That was the Red Arrows!' I declared with a smile. The alien nodded enthusiastically. 'Did you think they might be your spaceship?'

He took a step back a pace and frowned indignantly, as if I'd just said something really dumb.

'So, you speak English?' I faltered, glimpsing his flat,

long-toed feet. He pulled a stiff upside-down smile, then gestured as if adjusting an invisible shower control. By this, I think he meant, 'A little.'

'Where do you come from?' I asked, my eyes following his trails of blue smoke upwards.

'*Eeek!*' screeched the alien in a strange echo, pointing to the sky.

'Of course!' I said smiling. 'I know all about the planets — got a poster in my room, and lots of books. D'you want to come and see? You could show me your home!'

I could barely believe my luck when the alien shrugged his shoulders and smiled shyly, as if to say, 'Why not?'

TWO

Dad was still in the shed and, judging by the thumps I could hear through the living room wall, Rory was practising diving into the ocean from the sofa. (Either that, or — another of his favourite games — playing Batman leaping from the Empire State Building to catch a baddy.) Mum was still out.

With the coast clear, and, as you might imagine, more than a little excited, I took my alien friend straight up the stairs to my bedroom.

As I opened the door my enormous map of the universe confronted us, hanging directly above my bed, on the opposite side of the room.

I realised at this point it was probably my interest in space (so often mocked by others) that had singled me out for this special visit from an extraterrestrial being. Suddenly I felt privileged. Proud beyond words.

Thinking of what my friends were probably doing at this precise moment, I also felt extremely smug.

'Here it is!' I cried confidently, scrambling onto my bed and diving towards the map. 'Now, where are you from?'

No 'Eeek' in reply. No already familiar pant of cool breath behind me. I looked around. To my horror the alien had vanished! Only thin air hovered in my doorway.

'Friend…where are you?' My heart beat furiously. Could I have imagined all this? Just then, to my delight, a puff of blue smoke rose from the foot of my bed, whereupon the alien stood up grinning from ear to ear — holding out my football boots!

'How do you do that?' I gasped, staring at the edges of his mouth. (I swear they *really were* touching his ears!) But my friend wasn't listening. Instead he was fiddling with the laces of the boots, echoing a low hum.

Still ignoring me, he sat down on my bed and started putting my boots on. I, meanwhile, began eagerly pointing at my map of the universe quoting the names of the planets, which had moons and how many, and trying to guess which outreach my friend might have come from.

My boots seemed to fit him perfectly, though did look pretty stupid on the end of a pair of knobbly kneed, spindly fluorescent green legs!

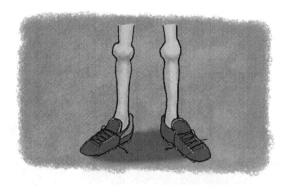

'Eeek', as I decided to call him, was now wandering around my room showing more interest in my football posters than any of my space stuff. He even tossed my Stargazer telescope aside in favour of my Northbridge United scarf, which he slung around his neck as he continued to rifle through the mess on my desk.

Finally I gave up my tour of the universe and scrambled off my bed. Eeek by now was sitting on the floor thumbing through the pages of my World Cup Sticker Book. When he reached the England team he suddenly stopped and his pale pink eyes filled with tears. Then a pear-shaped drop of water rolled down over his glowing green cheek and landed 'Splat!' right on Joe Carraber's head.

'Hey! Be careful with that!' I lunged forward. Immediately I regretted my outburst, for as I now clutched the book to my chest I could see more and more tears welling in my friend's eyes and, within moments, Eeek was rolling around on the carpet in a near puddle of water, sobbing with a strange echo.

'Look, Eeek, what is it?' I said with a sigh. This alien thing wasn't turning out to be half the fun I'd hoped. Let's face it, what self-respecting 11-year-old wants to spend their Saturday morning with a *crying* alien?

Eeek slowly gathered himself together and wiped away his remaining tears. He then gestured for the book, which I handed over — not without trepidation.

Eeek placed the book on the carpet and eagerly pointed at the sticker of Northbridge United and England striker, Steve Mitchell.

'Steve Mitchell!' I said with a smile. Eeek nodded enthusiastically. 'Great player!' I added. Eeek clapped his hands. Now we were getting somewhere. 'Hang on? You *know* about Steve Mitchell?' I was talking to *an alien* after all!

Eeek confronted me with another of his indignant frowns.

'Nasty ankle injury,' I muttered vacantly. 'I hope he's okay for England-Brazil on Friday!'

To my horror, Eeek's eyes immediately began glistening again. 'Oh no, Eeek, please! No more crying!'

I now had my sanity to think of — not to mention my sodden carpet.

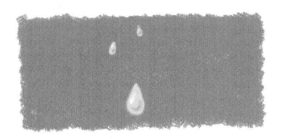

I was glad of my outburst, despite his tears, because Eeek suddenly pulled himself together, jumped up and started practising air kicks in front of my mirror.

'So!' I said. 'You know about the World Cup and the England Football Team! What else do you know about?'

Eeek gave a knowing wink, then climbed onto the middle of my bed and crossed his spindly legs. A glazed look came over his eyes as he now pointed at his tummy and started rubbing it as he hummed in a high pitch.

'Oh dear, you're hungry!' I said, now wondering what aliens ate for lunch.

Eeek shook his head impatiently then pointed to his tummy again as if to say, 'Look!'

I stared hard at the spot where his belly button should have been, but wasn't. Next thing a rectangle began drawing itself into his translucent green skin. I gasped in horror. *'Oh my God! You're a Teletubbie, aren't you? I'm on "You've Been Framed!" aren't I?'* How would I ever live this one down!

Eeek instantly raised his pale pink eyes to the ceiling, then tossed me a cool glance as if to say, 'Boy you really *are* dumb!' He then pointed impatiently at the rectangle in his tummy, which by now was opening like a sideways cat flap.

As the door into Eeek's tummy opened wider, so too did my mouth.

By the time Eeek started reaching *inside* his tummy, I swear, my bottom jaw was all but on the duvet where I sat opposite him.

'What on *earth* are you doing?' I shrieked, fully expecting a blood-soaked intestine to flop out at any moment. (My mum's face on seeing a blood- soaked duvet, along with me and an alien on it, wasn't far from my mind either.)

Eeek echoed a chuckle, and carried on smiling and shaking his head knowingly as his frail green arm reached deeper and deeper inside his tummy. I was now waiting for his hand to appear out the other side of his back, like a scene from a late night horror film, but it somehow didn't.

'*Eeeeeek!*' he finally squealed, as though he'd found what he'd been looking for.

My friendly green alien then yanked his hand out and dropped a small purple glowing case onto my bed. It looked a bit like a little lunch box.

The small door in his tummy then conveniently closed itself and disappeared.

End of sample — We hope you had fun!

You can order *Eeek! The Runaway Alien* online or from your local bookshop. And if you'd like an *Eeek!* school visit, ask your teacher to get in touch :)

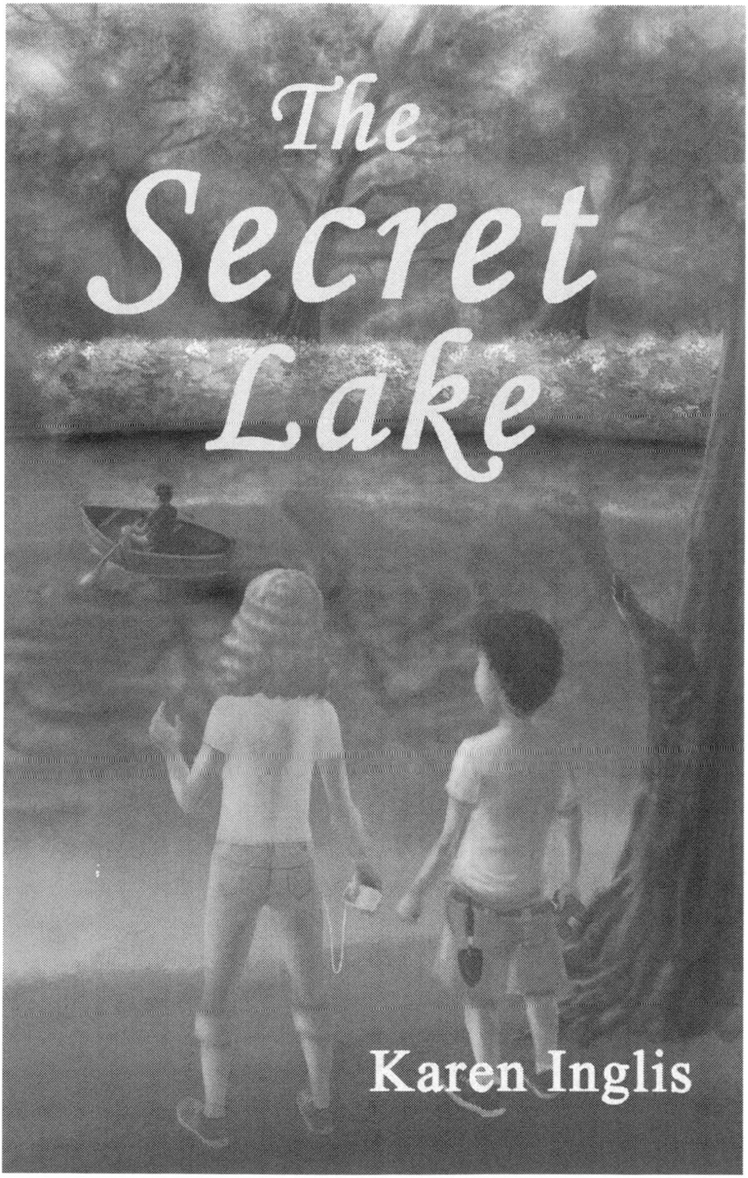
The Secret Lake
Karen Inglis

1 ~ THE GARDENER

Tom's face felt so hot he was sure it was about to explode. The midday sun beat down mercilessly on his back, and the beads of sweat that had long since formed on his forehead began to itch and tickle. But still he dug on. Surely if he kept going there would be a sign. A tuft of silky fur perhaps? A distant squeak? Or (and this really would be the best!) a pair of tiny eyes squinting blindly up towards the daylight.

He paused to wipe the trickling sweat with the back of his wrist, then lifted his spade for what felt like the one hundredth time — just as a dark shadow loomed up from behind. A familiar chill travelled down his spine as, with heart pounding, he swivelled round to meet the piercing stare of the gardener, Charlie Green.

'Now look 'ere, Tom Hawken, I've told you before,

I've enough trouble chasing up these darn molehills without 'avin' you goin' round diggin' 'em up.'

Tom felt his cheeks burning which was odd because his body was suddenly freezing. Charlie Green had had it in for him since the day they had moved to the gardens, of that he was sure. He was always giving him funny looks.

Tom tried to speak, but his throat, which suddenly felt drier than the Sahara at noon, stuck tight. He never had been brilliant at getting out of trouble — just expert at getting into it.

Charlie Green squinted darkly. 'Next time, I'll 'ave to tell yer mum!' he growled. 'Now, take that rag o' yours and be off.'

Tom fumbled as he gathered up the corners of his Treasure Rag. To his relief, Charlie Green hadn't noticed the array of plant bulbs he had dug up, which now lay scattered in amongst his 'earth treasure' — three handsome stones, a piece of broken green bottle and a tatty old purse that had probably belonged to a child's doll. The stones he would keep and place in his box marked 'Tom's Earth Treasure', which sat in the grate of his enormous bedroom fireplace. Everything else he would throw back.

By the time he nudged open the small gate separating his parents' small patio garden from the main communal gardens Charlie Green had already re-filled the mole hole and was now stomping angrily across the lawns towards his shed. Clusters of tiny earth mounds lay scattered all around; it had been a bad week for moles in West London.

———

Tom's heart still took off every time he entered his first floor bedroom: after his tiny room in their tenth floor Hong Kong apartment it really was a dream come true! His ceiling reached high, like a private indoor sky; the narrow French doors, opening onto the tiny sun-filled balcony, stood tall as skyscrapers, and on the far wall a magnificent marble fireplace stood even taller than he was. But, more important than all of these things, was the view. Tom's new room looked out onto a vast rambling garden that stretched as far as the eye could see. The garden, which was shared by all of the houses in the square, was filled with clusters of rhododendron bushes and sprawling oak trees whose branches seemed to brush the passing clouds.

Tom pressed his nose hard against the French door window and breathed in deeply, still wondering about Charlie Green. Then, through his clouds of warm breath on the glass, he saw a small dog shoot out from a cluster of trees and race across the lawn towards the houses. Slowly, Tom's mouth widened into a grin. 'I DON'T BELIEVE IT, STELL!' he yelled at the top of his voice. 'HARRY'S BACK!'

Stella, who was lying on her bed in her room next door studying her friendship bracelet, didn't answer. With her iPhone music on full volume, she was busy hoping that her friends back in Hong Kong, who would all be asleep now, had thought about her today. She also happened to be crunching her fifth fruit polo of the day — lime-green flavour to be precise — the one that always made her ears tingle. 'Tom thinks he's in heaven,' she had just messaged her best friend, Hannah, on Facebook. 'But it's so deathly dull here — all molehills and boys!'

Stella didn't budge. Nor, for that matter, did Tom who was now leaning out so far over his balcony he was in danger of falling off. He was determined to see if old Mrs Moon would be at her gate to welcome her disappearing dog. Of course she wasn't. After all, she would have to be psychic to know exactly *when* Harry would choose to come home. Never mind psychic, all the garden residents thought Mrs Moon was batty. Her 'Lost Dog' notices were pinned up everywhere and she drove them all mad phoning them up each time Harry went off, which was often for days at a time.

Tom had found himself wondering about Harry when he was out digging. The little long-haired terrier's comings and goings seemed to be part of garden life — as did the snarling Charlie Green and the molehills and, of course, the dotty old Mrs Moon. But why did the dog keep disappearing? And exactly where did he go? As thoughts of Charlie Green quickly evaporated, Tom resolved to solve Harry's mystery by summer's end.

2 ~ BENEATH THE MOUND

'I wonder where Harry's gone this time,' Stella murmured as the sound of their mother's piano playing wafted through the morning breeze. Harry had been missing for almost a week and Mrs Moon was beside herself. (As a result, so were most of the garden residents.)

Tom and Stella were sitting on their favourite mound of grass on 'The Island'. The Island was a cluster of four oak trees in the centre of the garden skirted by rhododendron bushes. Stella twirled her friendship bracelet — a present from Hannah when they had left. 'Neither time nor distance will break our bond,' Hannah had said dramatically when she'd given it to her. How much those words meant now!

'I wonder where Harry goes *every* time,' Tom said

with a frown as he picked at the mound of grass with his trowel.

'Don't do that!' snapped Stella. 'If Charlie Green catches you you'll be—'

'*HEY! What's this?*' Tom's eyes locked open as he sat staring between his legs at the ground.

'What's *what?*' Stella leaned forward as Tom continued scraping grass off the top of the mound beneath him.

'I think it's real treasure!' he shrieked. Sure enough, as Tom carried on digging, and his eyes continued to widen, underneath they could see what looked like the rounded lid of a wooden container — a real treasure chest.

Suddenly Stella clutched Tom's arm. 'Ouch! Let go, will you!' he squealed.

'*Shh..!*' hissed Stella, sitting bolt up and staring straight ahead. The bushes opposite rustled. Stella and Tom sat still as statues. If Charlie Green appeared now they were done for.

'Must have been a bird,' whispered Tom, finally letting out a breath. The bush was still again. He looked down and carried on digging. 'It's a box, and it's got grooves on the lid!' he gasped. The rounded lid of the treasure chest seemed to go on forever as the patch Tom dug grew wider and wider.

And then Stella's pale blue eyes widened.

'Tom!' she whispered in disbelief. 'It's not a box! It's a *boat!*'

'A boat!' said Tom. 'It can't be a boat, stupid, there's no water around here!'

At that moment the bush opposite trembled violently. They really had had it this time; they knew Charlie Green's breathless snort anywhere. He was probably crawling through the undergrowth to take them by surprise.

Then, with a final sharp rustle, the leaves ahead parted and out into the clearing appeared... Harry.

'Harry!' they cried.

'He's *soaking!*' exclaimed Stella.

Harry took one look at Tom and Stella, then turned towards home and fled.

'Wait, Harry!' Tom began to take chase. But it was too late. Harry streaked like lightening out past the rhododendron bushes and across the sun-drenched lawn. Mrs Moon didn't know it yet, but she was in for a very pleasant surprise.

'Tom, *come back!*'

Tom gave up his chase about half way across the lawn, just as their mother's voice echoed across the garden. 'Tom, Stella! Come on! We're leaving!'

'Help me with this.' Stella was dragging a log across

the lawn towards the mound. 'If Charlie Green finds this mess we'll be grounded indoors for a week!'

Tom looked despondent. He had just unearthed the greatest treasure of his digging career and here he was being told he had to cover it up again.

'But I want to get the boat out!' he protested.

'We haven't got time! We're going to grandma's!' said Stella breathlessly. 'Quick, take that end.'

They shuffled three or four steps sideways and lowered the log down on top of the mound.

Tom stepped back and kicked the log in frustration.

'Look,' said Stella firmly, 'it's no use making a fuss now. We'll come back tomorrow and see if we can find out where Harry came from.'

Tom's face twisted into a puzzled frown. 'What do you mean by that?'

'Well,' said Stella, tearing at the wrapping of her sweet packet, 'where there's a boat there must be water.'

She popped an orange polo into her mouth and raised her eyebrows in excitement. '*I* think Harry knows where that water is — and it's *somewhere around here!*'

End of sample

We hope you've enjoyed the story so far :)
*Order **The Secret Lake** from your local bookshop or online*

JOIN KAREN'S READERS' CLUB

GET FREE POSTERS, SNEAK PREVIEWS AND MORE!

Ask a grown-up to sign up for you to get:

- Free artwork and posters from Karen's books
- 'Sneak peek' previews of works in progress (story excerpts, illustrations, book covers)
- The chance to request advance review copies of Karen's upcoming books
- The chance to give feedback on character names, book covers, titles, story ideas
- Advance notice of special offers, book launches and author events
- Karen's latest reading and recommendations of other great children's books

Find out more at
kareninglisauthor.com/readers-club

WALTER BROWN — MAGICAL THANKS

With thanks to Bridget Rendell and Debbie Young for reading early drafts of Walter Brown and offering invaluable feedback, and to Melissa Hyder for helping me take the final draft one step further.

Also my huge thanks to Harlan, Ike and Fraser and to the team of six boys at St Anthony's Prep for reading Walter and giving me your feedback.

Finally, thank you once again to my illustrator Damir Kundalić for bringing my story to life.